MEET ALL THESE FRIENDS IN BUZZ BOOKS:

Thomas the Tank Engine
The Animals of Farthing Wood
James Bond Junior
Fireman Sam
Joshua Jones
Bugs Bunny
Flintstones
Rupert
Babar

First published in Great Britain 1993
by Buzz Books, an imprint of Reed Children's Books
Michelin House, 81 Fulham Road, London SW3 6RB
and Auckland, Melbourne, Singapore and Toronto

ISBN 1 85591 287 2

Printed in Italy by Olivotto

Barbella's Revenge

Story adapted by Caryn Jenner

Illustrations by Arkadia

"You're history, Nick Nack!" said James Bond Junior.

He'd already chased the notorious villain through the terminal at Heathrow Airport, and now it looked as if he'd finally caught him at the security X-ray machine.

But Nick Nack just laughed. "You'll never catch me, Bond!" he declared as he scrambled onto the conveyor and over the X-ray machine.

You won't get away, Nick Nack!

When James reached the conveyor,
all that was left of Nick Nack was his
walkie-talkie.

"That scoundrel must have dropped this,"
thought James. "Perhaps it will give us a
clue to what he's got up his sleeve."

James's friend, I.Q., was waiting for him on the airport observation deck.

"Can you fix this, I.Q.?" asked James, handing him the walkie-talkie. "It doesn't seem to work."

"It's security-locked," I.Q. replied.

He disconnected some wires and a few minutes later a woman's voice came over the walkie-talkie.

"I'll see you at the crime conference in Rio de Janeiro, S.C.U.M. Lord."

"That's Barbella!" exclaimed James.

"Then we'll decide where to drop Asteroid 604," Barbella was saying. "Kaboom!"

"Well, I.Q.," said James, "do you fancy spending half-term in Brazil?"

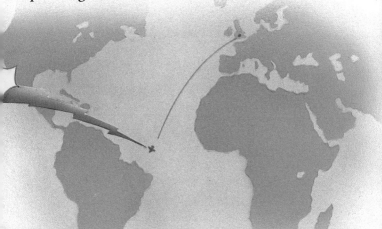

In Rio, I.Q. decided to work on some new
gadgets while James rang his friend,
Carmen Marimba. Carmen met James on
the landing pad on the roof of the hotel,
and soon they were flying above the city in
her helicopter searching for Barbella.

But Barbella and Nick Nack had already spotted James from their headquarters deep in the Brazilian jungle.

"Nick Nack, prepare the magnetic cannon," Barbella ordered, glaring at James' image on her monitor.

"Locked on target," said Nick Nack.

Barbella fired, then watched the monitor gleefully as a powerful magnetic beam hit Carmen's helicopter.

Suddenly, the helicopter began to spin out of control as the magnetic beam pulled it rapidly towards the ground.

"We're losing altitude," said Carmen.
"Get ready for a crash landing!"

"Not yet!" James declared. He was fiddling intently with a knob on his watch.

Suddenly, the helicopter levelled off, skimming safely over the outskirts of Rio.

"This is the magnetic watch that I.Q. invented," James explained. "I've adjusted the polarity to repel the force of Barbella's magnetic cannon. I'll have to tell I.Q. that his watch is a great success — although it is a few minutes fast."

But S.C.U.M. Lord, it's my cannon.

"James Bond Junior is still alive!"
S.C.U.M. Lord told Barbella.

"But we shot the 'copter out of the air
with the magnetic cannon," Barbella
protested. "I saw it go down."

"Well, he landed safely," said S.C.U.M.
Lord. "After the crime conference, I will
take charge of the magnetic cannon."

13

Back at the hotel, I.Q. showed James his latest gadgets.

"This ring contains compressed air," he said. "Just attach it to the regulator in this pen and breathe."

"Breath fresheners!" James exclaimed, picking up a tube of mints.

"In actual fact," said I.Q., "that is a sound amplifier. You'll be able to hear through walls or doors, or almost anything..."

Unfortunately, James didn't hear Barbella's latest scheme.

"S.C.U.M. Lord thinks he's so cool. Well, he's going to be burning up when I drop that asteroid on *him*!" Barbella said. "I'll program the cannon to bring down Asteroid 604 on Rio de Janeiro!"

"But what about us?" asked Nick Nack.

"We'll be gone before the asteroid hits, don't worry," said Barbella with an evil grin.

That evening, James eavesdropped on the crime conference. He perched on a building platform ten floors above the famous Carnival in Rio, holding I.Q.'s mint amplifier to the window.

"I thought I'd find you here, Bond," said a familiar voice, and it wasn't coming through the amplifier!

James spun around to find Nick Nack hovering in the air with a jet pack, his laser gun pointing straight at James!

James leaped, grabbing hold of Nick Nack's ankles at the same time as he knocked the gun out of his hands.

"Let go! The jet pack won't carry two!" yelled Nick Nack. "We'll fall...!"

But James clung on tightly as they fell
toward the carnival below. Then suddenly,
a gust of wind caught the pair and blew
them across the street!

Nick Nack started wriggling his legs and
kicking wildly. James knew he couldn't
hold on much longer. As the wind carried
them over the harbour, James let go.

Nick Nack screamed with laughter. "Good
riddance, Bond!"

18

James held his breath as he splashed into the cool, dark water. The impact stunned him for a moment and he sank deep into the ocean.

"I wasn't really in the mood for deep sea diving tonight," he said to himself.

Quickly, James attached I.Q.'s ring to the regulator pen to release the compressed air. He took a gulp of oxygen, then made his way to the surface.

When James returned to the hotel, I.Q. showed him a heat photograph of the jungle.

"This dark blotch is Barbella's headquarters."

"Let's go!" James exclaimed as he led the way to Carmen's helicopter.

Carmen landed in a clearing and the three friends scrambled through the dark jungle.

"Come on, I.Q. Hurry," urged James.

"But s-something's s-slithering around my neck," said I.Q. "I think it's a giant s-snake!"

20

James and Carmen struggled to free I.Q. from the grasp of the giant anaconda, but the snake's grip was too tight.

"We'll stun the snake with sound," said James, pressing his mint amplifier to the snake's head. "LET GO!" he yelled.

Immediately, the snake released I.Q. and dropped to the ground in shock.

"Shall we take our ssslithery friend to visit Barbella?" James suggested.

Inside Barbella's headquarters, James let
the snake go. As it slithered over a pressure
plate on the floor, an alarm sounded.

James, I.Q. and Carmen ducked out of
sight as Nick Nack appeared. The anaconda
rose up from the floor and lunged at him.

A horrified Barbella watched on her
monitor as the snake quickly wrapped itself
around Nick Nack's body until only his toes
and the top of his head were showing.

She rushed into the corridor, leaving her control room unlocked. James and his friends darted inside and bolted the door.

I.Q. examined the control panel. "Asteroid 604 is due to hit Rio in fifteen minutes!"

"Can you stop it?" asked James.

"I'll certainly try," I.Q. replied.

Suddenly, there was a loud pounding at the door.

"I know you're in there, Bond," Barbella bellowed. "Open up or I'll punch and I'll kick, and I'll smash this door down!"

"Can you hurry up a bit, I.Q?" said James as his friend worked frantically at the control panel.

Counting down five minutes.

"Look out!" yelled Carmen as the door splintered, revealing a very angry Barbella.

"Get out of here, Bond!" she thundered, charging at James.

"I've done it!" I.Q. interrupted. "I've reprogrammed the magnetic cannon. Asteroid 604 should hit us in five minutes."

"Five minutes!" echoed James in disbelief.

"We've got to save Rio!" James exclaimed.

"Come on," said I.Q. calmly. "Let's go and watch the asteroid."

Nervously, James and Carmen followed I.Q. outside. They looked into the sky, where a huge sizzling mass was rapidly approaching. The flames lit up two distant figures flying away on their jet packs.

"You see," I.Q. explained. "I increased the power of the magnetic cannon, thereby speeding up the asteroid so that most of it burns away as it shoots through the atmosphere. By the time the asteroid lands, it will be the size of a golf ball."

At that moment, the asteroid fizzled out and a smoking rock dropped from the sky.

Watch out!

Don't worry, James.

James was back at school, sitting through one of Mr Milbanks' boring science lectures.

"Astronomy is the study of heavenly bodies, such as stars, planets, comets, asteroids…" droned Mr Milbanks.

James tried to cover a yawn.

"Pay attention, Bond," Mr Milbanks scolded. "You'll be expected to do a research project on this lesson."

"I.Q. and I will do our project on asteroids," said James. "In fact, we've already done some research."

He handed the burnt-out asteroid to the astonished headmaster. "How very interesting," said Mr Milbanks. "You can have extra marks for this."

"Thank you, Sir," said James. "And thank you, Barbella!" he thought.

29